# Father Fox's Christmas Rhymes

## Clyde Watson
### Pictures by Wendy Watson

FARRAR STRAUS GIROUX

NEW YORK

Text copyright © 2003 by Clyde Watson
Illustrations copyright © 2003 by Wendy Watson
All rights reserved
Distributed in Canada by Douglas & McIntyre Ltd.
Printed and bound in China by South China Printing Company Limited
First edition, 2003
1   3   5   7   9   10   8   6   4   2

Library of Congress Cataloging-in-Publication Data
Watson, Clyde.
    Father Fox's Christmas rhymes / Clyde Watson ; pictures by Wendy Watson.
        p.   cm.
    Summary: Illustrated verses follow the activities of Father Fox and his family
as they prepare for Christmas.
    ISBN 0-374-37576-3
    1. Christmas—Juvenile poetry.  2. Children's poetry, American.  [1. Christmas—Poetry.
2. American poetry.]  I. Watson, Wendy, ill.  II.  Title.

PS3573.A8485 T55 2003
811'.54—dc21

2002075200

*This book is for*
*Julia & Polly*
*& Forrest & Holly!*

AND FOR B.L.—
FOR POKING,
BLOWING PUFFS
OF AIR,
& FANNING!

Here am I, old Father Fox
With sweets in my pocket & holes in my socks
Bringing a basket brimful of cheer
A toy for each day until Christmas is here

Little wild snow horse
Eyes shining black
Tail made of twigs
& the wind at your back

Up into the saddle
Holding tight to your mane
I'll gallop to the North Pole
& come right back again

Secret things in
Secret places
Whispered words
& knowing faces

Red glass beads
In the cracks of the floor
A whiff of paint
From behind a door

Paper rustles
Scissors snip
A telltale wink
& a finger to the lip

Through the forest deep & still
Let's go wandering as we will
With snowflakes floating gently round
& tracks of deer upon the ground

Here it is, the perfect tree
A prettier sight there cannot be
It stands majestic with the rest
Trimmed just with snow & a small bird's nest

Fresh apple cider
& slices of orange
All in a great big pot
With a cinnamon stick
& three whole cloves
Simmered till piping hot!

Candle fire, precious light
Earth-bound star in dark of night
Flickering, sinking, wavering, winking
Bravely burning on . . .

Let us each one bring a candle
Walk together & shining forth
Become a stream, a river, a sea
Of dancing stars in harmony

With eyes so wise
& a trusting heart
& a spirit that sings like a dove

Although you are little
You're more than enough
A sweet little plenty of love

The kitchen is bursting with uncles & aunts
With buttery fingers & floury pants
Mixing & mincing & stirring & such
For puddings & pies that we mustn't touch

So let's set the table up fancy & fine
With candles & napkins & goblets that shine
A basket of holly, a bowl full of pears
& last but not least all the benches & chairs

Finally we sit up & down the big table
Glad to hold hands & be still, if we're able
Then lifting our heads we smile & begin
Little Polly's already got grease on her chin!

Clouds in heaven, hear our call:
Over the land let snowflakes fall
Soft & silver, feathery bright
Snow like diamonds in the night
Snow on snow till when we rise
The world all white shall greet our eyes

The hour is late

Now off to bed

Because Santa won't come till you sleep

So pull up the covers

& close your eyes

But quiet—don't make a peep

You might hear footsteps
Up on the roof
Or a soft little jingling bell
For Christmas Eve
Is a magical time
& you NEVER can tell!

*Star light, star bright*
*The first star I see tonight*
*I wish I may, I wish I might*
*Have the wish I wish tonight*

I wish that all who see this star
Wherever on the earth they are
Would make one wish for the world tonight
All of us together with our eyes shut tight:

A wish for peace & love & joy
More precious things than any toy
There is enough, if we will share
For every creature, everywhere

Stoke the fire
Bright & warm
Against the dark
Of winter's storm
No matter how fiercely
The wind may blow
Lashing the window
With ice & snow
These flames that crackle
Lick & dart
Will toast the toes
& warm the heart

Listen! Sh-h! Hush, my love
What is it that I hear?
The voices of angels far away
But slowly coming near

Up the road & around the corner
Singing through the snow
Right to my door with a song still as sweet
Tonight as it was long ago

Christmas is here, come quickly with me
To fly down the stairs & in to the tree
Where apples & candies & tiny wrapped things
Are twisting & turning on fine golden strings
Every branch full of promise & light & surprise
Sing Christmas, O Christmas right up to the skies!

*Christmas is all but over now*

*There's nothing left under the tree*

*Except wait! Over here there's one more present,*

*& the tag says . . . it's for me!*